AN ANASAZI WELCOME

Written by **KAY MATTHEWS**

Illustrated by **BARBARA BELKNAP**

RED CRANE BOOKS

First Edition

Printed in Korea

Typography by Jim Mafchir
Cover and text illustrations by Barbara Belknap

Library of Congress Cataloging-in-Publication Data

Matthews, Kay.
     An Anasazi welcome / written by Kay Matthews ; illustrated by
Barbara Belknap. — 1st ed.
          p.   cm.
     Summary: When his family moves from the East to build a home in
the Southwest desert, Gramps makes a deal with an Anasazi ghost to
help them learn to live in harmony with the land.
     ISBN 1-878610-27-9 (pbk.) :
     [1. Grandfathers—Fiction. 2. Ghosts—Fiction. 3. Pueblo
Indians—Fiction. 4. Indians of North America—Southwest. New—
Fiction. 5. Southwest, New—Fiction.] I. Belknap, Barbara, ill.
II. Title.
PZ7.M4336An 1992
[Fic]—dc20   92-796
                                                                    CIP
                                                                    AC

Red Crane Books
826 Camino de Monte Rey
Santa Fe, New Mexico 87501

GLOSSARY

Adobe: A sun-dried brick made of mud and straw

Anasazi: Navajo word for the ancestors of the present day
Pueblo Indian

Ancestral: Belonging to your ancestor (a relative who lived
before you)

Chile: A hot pepper used in cooking

Hispanic: A person whose ancestors were Spanish

Piñon nut: A small nutlike seed that comes from the piñon
pine tree

Viga: A round ceiling beam made from an evergreen tree

"**A**re we really going to live here?" Nora asked.

"In the middle of the desert?" complained her sister, Maud.

"This may be the desert, girls," said their father Sam, "but it's one of the prettiest places I've ever been. Look at those mountains. They'll be right outside our living room window. Look up at the sky. Have you ever seen a sky as blue as that?"

"And what about Gramps?" Nora asked.

"Is he going to live here with us?" Maud wanted to know.

Gramps was the family oddball. He wandered around talking to himself in the middle of the night and ate popcorn whenever he felt like it, even before breakfast.

"Gramps is too old to live by himself," explained their mother, Katie. "We're going to build a house with enough room for all of us."

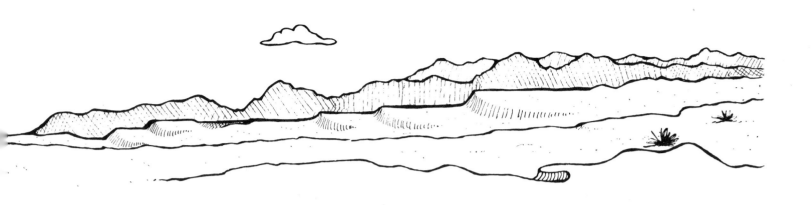

Nora and Maud rolled their eyes at their parents. They'd made them leave all their friends back East and move to this strange place where plants had thorns, not leaves, and instead of grass there were rocks and sand. Now they had to live with their crazy grandfather. They were *not* enthusiastic.

Gramps wasn't all that enthusiastic about living with them either. He'd moved away from *his* friends back East twenty years before to live in a Hispanic village not far from the new house site. Once his children were grown, he had decided it was time to live where he'd always wanted to live, in the high mountain desert where there was space to breathe. His small adobe house was over a hundred years old, with cracked walls, uneven floors, and a roof that leaked dirt. But it suited him just fine.

"At least I got my pickin's of land for the new house," he grumbled to himself. "I can still see my mountains and red mesas and blue sky." Gramps walked along the trench that the man with the backhoe had just dug, where the concrete would be poured to support the walls of the house. "Sam and Katie don't know beans

about building an adobe house," he continued, taking out his measuring tape. "I'm going to have to make sure they do it right. I've learned a thing or two from watching my neighbors work on *their* houses."

"Ouch!" something yelled as he poked the tape down to the bottom of the trench.

Gramps stood up, startled. "Tie me to an anthill and scatter my bones! Now I'm hearing things," he exclaimed. He walked a little way along the trench and again started to measure.

"Will you kindly stop poking me," the voice demanded. "I haven't done anything to bother you, but look what you're doing to my home!"

"Are you talking to me?" Gramps asked, looking at the ground.

"Since when can dirt talk?"

"I am of the earth but also the mountains, streams, sky, and trees," the voice answered, and suddenly, there in front of Gramps was a ghost with long, black, braided hair.

"Tarnation—you're an Indian!" Gramps declared.

"What would you expect, a penguin?" the ghost grinned. "Anasazis live in the desert, penguins on ice."

"Anasazis?" Gramps questioned.

"The ancient ones," the ghost explained. "And I'm not happy that you're building your house on this spot. My people lived here hundreds of years ago. Why aren't your children moving into your house like we did with our parents?"

"We don't do that anymore," Gramps said sadly. "Young whippersnappers don't think old folks are good for anything."

"Well, in that case, Grandfather, maybe we can teach them a thing or two," the ghost smiled. "I think I'll haunt this place."

"By crackey *that's* an idea," Gramps laughed. "But don't go scarin' 'em too much."

"I'll make you a deal, Grandfather," the ghost said. "You make sure this house is built right, like the ancient ones did, with respect for the earth and trees and animals. In return, I'll go easy on them."

As the ghost started to sink into the ground Gramps yelled, "Wait just a flea bitin' second. How can I get a'hold of you?"

"Just call Eya, and I'll be heeeeeere," she called back and was gone.

9

"My, my, my," exclaimed Buela Bullsnake, slithering along the sand in the hot sun. "Look, children, at that lovely pile of adobesss," she hissed. "Adobesss make a wonderful home. They're made of mud and ssstraw, then baked into bricksss in the sssun. When it's hot outside they hold the coolnesss of the night air, and when it's cold they trap the sssun and keep you warm."

"Were they left here for usss?" the six little bullsnakes asked.

"No, children. Not much in this world is left for sssnakes. They're here for a human'sss house, but we're going to find a nice place to live at the bottom of the pile where no one will sssee usss."

"What are humansss?" the six little bullsnakes asked.

"Humans are not very nice to snakes," interrupted the ghost, bowing in the air to introduce

herself. "I'm Eya, an Anasazi ghost. Welcome to my ancestral home."

"Pleasssed to meet you, Eya," Buela Bull-snake said. "It's our ancestral home, too. My relativesss all lived on thisss land."

"Then rest assured you'll be treated with kindness while you're here in the adobe pile," Eya promised. "Maybe once in a while you could come out and slither around so the humans can see you? I'm trying to teach them respect for the land—and snakes!"

"We'll do our partsss, won't we children?" Buela Bullsnake hissed.

"This is going to be more fun than I thought," Eya laughed and disappeared.

11

Sam, Katie, Maud, Nora, and Gramps had been laying adobes all day and were resting in the sand.

"I've worked harder today than I have in my entire life," Katie sighed.

"And the walls are only knee high!" Sam complained.

The girls were too tired to talk. Gramps sat next to them, eating his popcorn. "I reckon we could use a hand around here," he said.

Suddenly, the walls behind them became a foot taller.

"Is that the kind of help you mean, Grandfather?" Eya called from behind the wall.

"Well chill my chiles!" Gramps exclaimed. "But shh," he whispered to Eya. "They'll hear you."

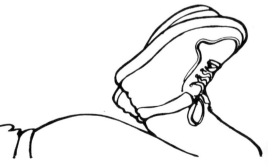

12

"Don't worry, you're the only one who knows I'm here," Eya explained. "By the way, have you met the snake family that lives under the adobe pile?"

"Great balls of fire!" Gramps yelled.

"Now don't get excited, Grandfather," Eya laughed. "They've got a right to be here, too."

"If they leave us alone, by gum, we'll leave them alone," Gramps offered.

"The idea is to learn to live happily together, Grandfather," Eya sighed. "Now how about a few more adobes for a good day's work?"

Again, the walls were a foot higher.

"Hey, everybody," Sam pointed. "I think we did more work than we thought!"

"I guess we did, Dad," Maud agreed.

"But when did we do it?" wondered Nora.

One hot morning Buela Bullsnake and her children came out to sun themselves on some rocks. "Sssee children," Buela said, pointing her head at the window frame. Sitting on the window ledge were two shiny green lizards. "Hello!" Buela Bullsnake called to them. "I'm Buela Bullsssnake. Who are you?"

"Lionel and Lola Lizard," Lola answered. "Oh, what darling children!" she exclaimed. "Lionel and I have none of our own, but we *love* children."

"Do you live here, too?" Lionel asked Buela Bullsnake. "We love living in this big window that catches all the sun and keeps us warm."

"Boo!" Eya exclaimed, appearing before them.

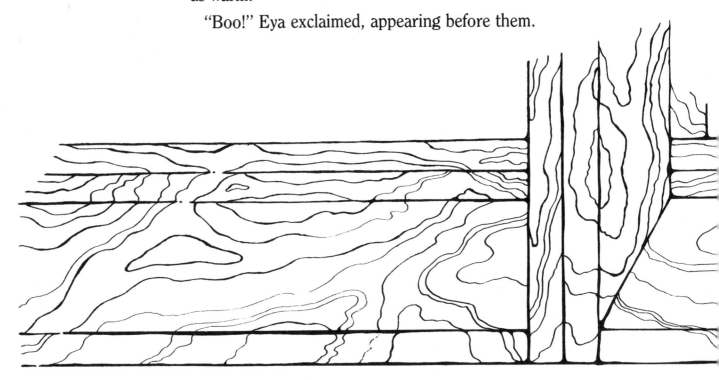

"Goodness gracious!" Lola Lizard cried and almost fell off the window.

"I've always wanted to see if I could really scare someone like that," Eya explained, settling onto the ledge next to them. "Nothing personal," she apologized to the lizards. "I'm Eya. Welcome to my house."

"We thought this was a human house," Lionel and Lola said.

"It is and I'm haunting it," the ghost smiled. "Are you planning on sticking around for all the excitement?"

"We think this is a great place to live," they said. "Lots of sun and good neighbors—and all these adorable children."

"The more the merrier," Eya said. "Welcome to the neighborhood—and the haunting!"

Soon the walls of the house were up, and the family was ready to put on the ceiling and roof. One day they all went to a tree cutting area in the mountains above the village and chose some tall ponderosa pine trees to use as ceiling beams, called vigas. Gramps made sure the loggers left plenty of other trees for the deer, mountain lions, bears, and squirrels who lived in the forest.

A huge truck brought the vigas to the house site. It took four men to unload them.

"Looks like we'll need some help to put these in place," Sam said.

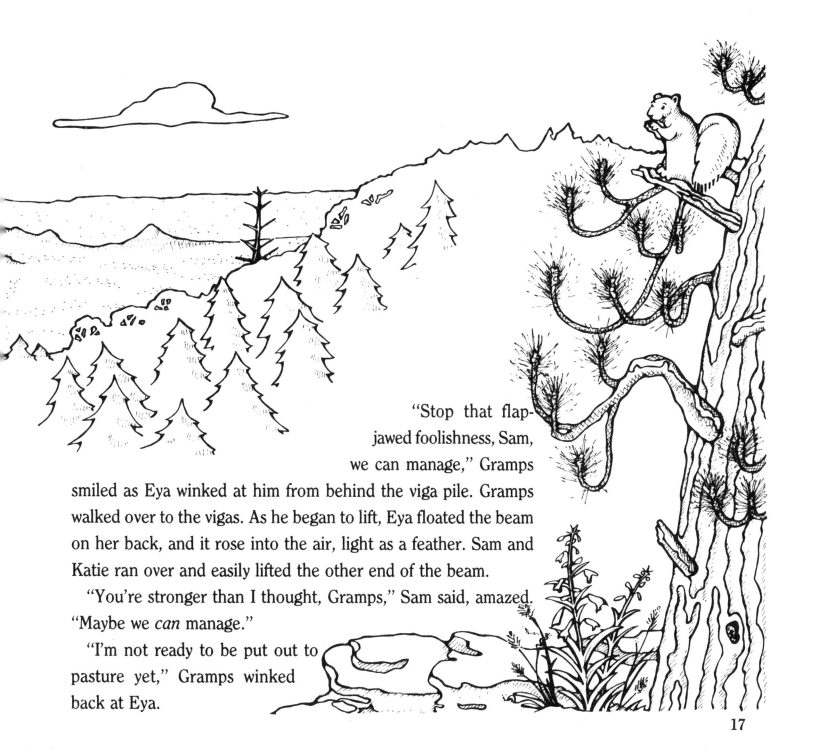

"Stop that flap-jawed foolishness, Sam, we can manage," Gramps smiled as Eya winked at him from behind the viga pile. Gramps walked over to the vigas. As he began to lift, Eya floated the beam on her back, and it rose into the air, light as a feather. Sam and Katie ran over and easily lifted the other end of the beam.

"You're stronger than I thought, Gramps," Sam said, amazed. "Maybe we *can* manage."

"I'm not ready to be put out to pasture yet," Gramps winked back at Eya.

While sunning themselves in the window one day, Lionel and Lola Lizard noticed two little gray birds flying in and out from under the new, shiny tin roof. They were carrying twigs, grass, and bits of feathers in their beaks.

"We have some new neighbors," Lionel nudged Lola. "And it looks like they're building a house, too."

"Oh, how exciting," Lola said. "Yoo-hoo, birds, can you introduce yourselves?"

"Twyla and Tommy Titmouse," they answered. "Sorry we can't stop to chat," Tommy said, "but we must finish the nest tonight so Twyla can lay her eggs tomorrow."

"Oh, we love babies," Lola exclaimed.

"Not to eat, I hope," Twyla chirped.

"Oh, no!" Lionel and Lola Lizard said, shocked. "We only eat flies."

Eya watched the birds make their nest under the eaves. "It may be sunny now," she said, "but when the rain finally comes to the desert they'll stay warm and dry."

"They seem like very nice birds," Lola said. "And they're going to have babies!"

Eya looked fondly at Lola. "We're getting to be a real family around here. I think it's time for some of us to meet the human family."

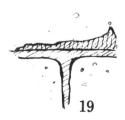

19

Gramps was building the adobe fireplace.

"Where did you learn how to make that kind of fireplace?" Eya asked, peeking over Gramps' shoulder.

"From my neighbor, José Griego," Gramps answered. "He's the best adobe fireplace maker there is. The Spanish people have used them for centuries to heat their houses."

"We all know a good thing when we see it. My people build them outside as ovens to bake bread," Eya added.

While Gramps worked, Nora and Maud carried red bricks one by one to their parents. They were laying them on sand for the living room floor. It was hard work, bending over on their knees, fitting bricks together in a zigzag pattern.

"Why don't they just use sssand as a floor?" Buela Bullsnake asked from her hiding place in the adobes. "Sssand is so sssoft and warm."

"Much too messy," Twyla Titmouse scolded from her nest.

"Bricks are nice and warm, too, after they've been in the sun for a while," Eya told them. "Now it's time for some tricks." She flew over the row of bricks Sam and Katie had just laid and quickly rearranged them.

Nora and Maud came in with more bricks and started giggling.

"What's so funny?" Katie asked. "I could use a laugh right now." She stared in disbelief at the floor. There, in the bricks, appeared the ghostly head of Eya.

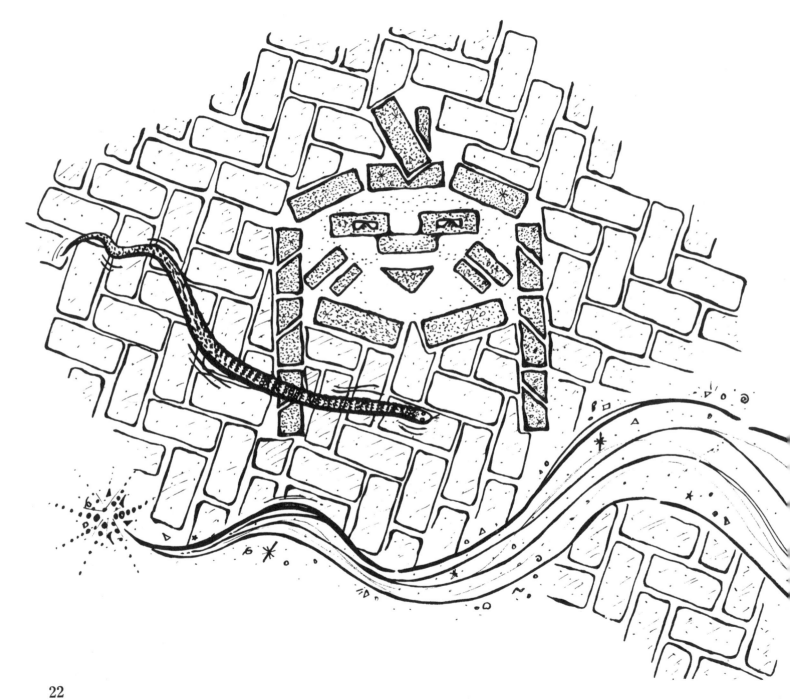

"Sam, Gramps, look!" she cried. "There's the shape of an Indian head in the bricks!"

"Great horny toads, did you do that, Katie?" Gramps wanted to know.

"Can we leave it like that?" the girls pleaded. "We like it!"

Just then Buela Bullsnake slithered across the room. Maud and Nora screamed and jumped back behind Gramps.

"It's a rattlesnake!" Katie screamed.

"Nope, just an old bullsnake," Gramps reassured her. "It won't hurt you." He shooed the girls back to work. "Just means less mice around here." Then, looking at the window where Eya was disappearing, he called out, "I reckon there's been enough excitement around here to make a coyote forget to howl."

Gramps sat in front of the fireplace, admiring his work. "Too bad its still hot as blazes outside or I'd give it a try," he muttered to himself.

"I bet Tyrone Tarantula is glad it's still hot," Eya called from above the fireplace. "Hate to tell him he'd have to move already."

"Tyrone Tarantula!" Gramps exclaimed. "Now we've got spiders livin' here too? Where's this little varmint?" He leaned over to look inside the chimney.

"Great place to look for cute spiders," a voice called out, as one hairy leg after another crawled out of the fireplace.

Gramps jumped back. "Tarnation! What're you goin' to do when it's winter and we're building fires here?" he demanded.

"I'm not all that particular," Tyrone replied. "If you plan on smoking me out, I can always move into the closet in somebody's shoe. . . ."

"Hold your horses, you mangy spider," Gramps growled.

"Everybody calm down," Eya laughed. "I thought we were one big happy family."

"Just what other critters are in this family besides snakes and spiders?" Gramps demanded.

"Some lizards and tufted titmice, for now," Eya replied. "Tyrone's not such a bad fellow. When he's not looking for a girlfriend, he can catch a few flies."

"As long as he doesn't set up housekeepin' in my boots," Gramps shuddered.

"Relax," Tyrone said, raising his hairy legs to admire them in the sunlight. "You think I'm going to live in someone's smelly old shoe? Don't you worry about me—I'll find a nice, cozy home when the time comes to move."

Up in the mountains the quaking aspen trees had turned brilliantly gold, and in the village the smell of roasting chiles and piñon nuts filled the valley as people prepared for winter. Sam, Katie, and the girls were excited at the thought of moving into a house they had made with their own hands and loving attention. Gramps hoped they'd be in before winter.

"It's looking pretty good, Grandfather," Eya observed.

"Not bad for a bunch of greenhorns, eh," Gramps laughed. "But we've got to get this house plastered before the snow flies, and I don't think we'll manage without some help. Know anyone who might do a little more work?"

"A ghost's work is never done," sighed Eya. "The sooner we get this house finished, the sooner I get to haunt it—weird noises in the night, lights turning on and off. . . . Remember our agreement?"

"I've lived up to my end of the bargain, partner," Gramps said.

"You *have* done a good job," Eya agreed. "You've built a house like the Anasazis did, and the Spanish after them, with rocks and mud from the earth and trees from the forests. You've come to accept the other creatures who also make their homes here. But most importantly, you've learned the history of this land and that respect for the land is also respect for the different kinds of people who have always lived here."

"I reckon that means you'll help us one more time?" Gramps grinned.

"At your service," Eya bowed.

The day before Halloween, the whole family moved into their new house. Eya decided it was time to call a meeting of all the animals out by the adobe pile. Gramps was invited, too.

"It's taken a long time, but our house is done and our humans are moved in," Eya said to the animals. "We've grown very fond of them, haven't we, friends?"

"It'sss very kind of you to leave thisss pile of adobes for me and the children," Buela Bullsnake said to Gramps.

"We love watching your adorable grandchildren from our sunny windowsill," Lionel and Lola Lizard said.

"Your strong tin roof keeps our babies snug and dry," Twyla and Tommy Titmouse added.

"Guess I should thank you for no fires in the fireplace yet," Tyrone Tarantula grumbled.

"Aw shucks, let's not go gettin' teary-eyed here," Gramps said, embarrassed. "I'm just livin' up to my end of the bargain."

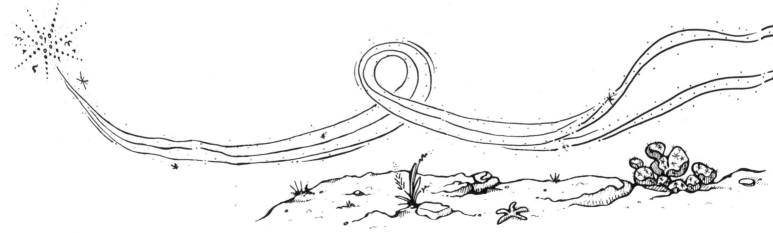

"Tomorrow is the perfect day to live up to *my* end of the bargain, eh, Grandfather? And everyone can play a part." Eya rose up off the adobe pile and called out, "Meeeeeet youuuuu aaaat midniiiiiight!" With that she was gone.

As the animals quietly crept away, Gramps looked at the beautiful house they had all built together and muttered proudly, "I may be crazy, talkin' to ghosts and animals, but that's a fair price for seein' this house finished and my family happy inside."

...Meeeeeet youuuuuu aaaat midniiiiiight !!!!!!!!!!!!

29

It was Halloween night, and Sam was ready to take the girls trick-or-treating. Then it started to rain. It rained and rained, until rivers of water poured off their new roof.

"Maud, Nora, I'm afraid we can't go," Sam said sadly. "I never thought I'd see this much rain in the desert."

"Back home everyone already has a million candy bars," Nora grumbled.

"We should never have moved here!" Maud cried.

Gramps gathered the girls in his arms. He said softly, "That rain pouring out of the sky tonight is our drinking and cleaning water, water that keeps our trees and flowers alive, water that the deer and rabbits, snakes and lizards, birds and spiders need to keep on goin'. But I've got a tornado of an idea. How about celebrating Halloween right here with the ghost who lives with us?"

"Oh, Gramps," the girls moaned. "You know there isn't any such thing as a ghost."

"Well, I declare," Gramps grinned, opening his bag of popcorn and pouring some into the girls' trick-or-treat bags. "Didn't I tell you that all *new* houses have ghosts that practice haunting for *old* houses?"

"Gramps!" the girls giggled, rolling their eyes.

"Let's turn out the lights and see if our ghost comes to haunt us," Katie suggested.

"I'll light a fire," Gramps called out in a voice loud enough for Tyrone to hear.

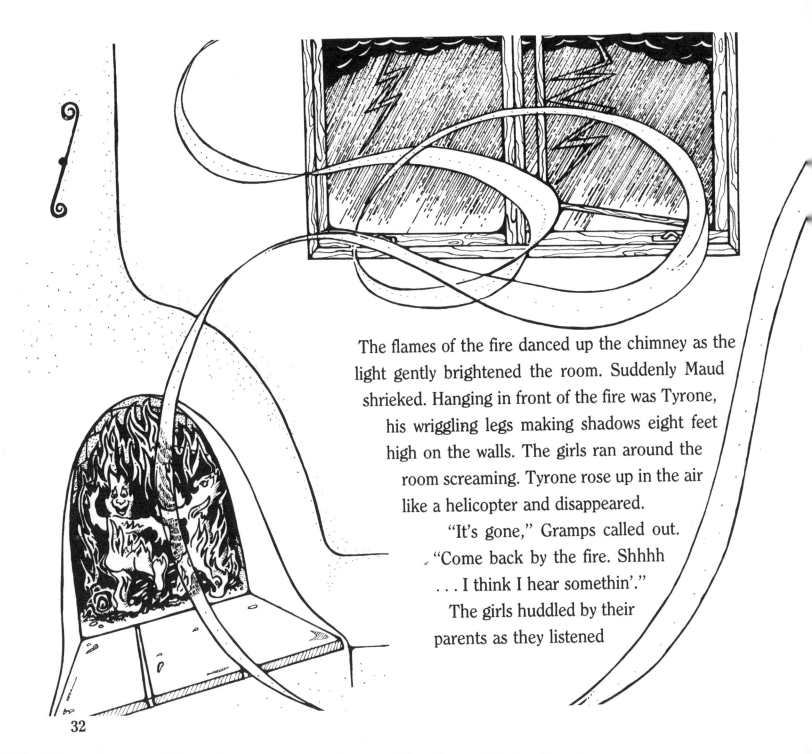

The flames of the fire danced up the chimney as the light gently brightened the room. Suddenly Maud shrieked. Hanging in front of the fire was Tyrone, his wriggling legs making shadows eight feet high on the walls. The girls ran around the room screaming. Tyrone rose up in the air like a helicopter and disappeared.

"It's gone," Gramps called out. "Come back by the fire. Shhhh ... I think I hear somethin'."

The girls huddled by their parents as they listened

to a low whistling sound coming from a corner of the room. Whoosh — through the air flew two dark creatures, dipping and diving. It was Tommy and Twyla Titmouse.

"It's bats, it's bats!" the girls cried, covering their eyes. Twyla and Tommy disappeared through an open window into the stormy night. "Are the bats gone?" Maud and Nora demanded, afraid to open their eyes.

"Hush!" Katie said, taking hold of Sam's hand. "Do you hear that rattling sound?"

"It's a ghost!" screamed the girls. Quick as lightning, Lionel and Lola Lizard jumped from the windowsill across Maud and Nora's heads, ruffling their hair, and landed on Gramps' shoulder. "It touched us!" they shrieked.

Gramps whispered to Lionel, "Is that Buela and the kids making all that racket?"

"They're under the furniture pretending to be ghosts," Lionel said.

Then the lights flicked on and off three times. In the brief instant of light, Gramps saw Eya hovering by the light switch.

"I am Eya, ghost of the Anasazi," a slow, trembling voice said. "Because you have built your house on my ancestral ground, you must do these things I ask. First, you must always respect the earth of which your house is made. Second, you must respect all the creatures that live with you on the earth for it is their home as much as yours. And third, you must only use what is necessary to live and never waste what the earth provides. With that, I welcome you to our home."

At that instant the lights came on, the fire died down, and the family sat blinking at each other. Gramps breathed a sigh of relief.

"Is it gone?" Maud whimpered.

"Was it really a ghost?" Nora asked.

"You'll have to ask Gramps that," Sam winked at his father. "That was quite a show, Gramps. We owe you a big thanks for saving Halloween."

"Eya gets all the credit for that," Gramps muttered, embarrassed. He sat down next to Maud and Nora. "What do you think that ghost was talking about, kids?"

"Well," Nora answered, "maybe the ghost was saying that all those spiders and snakes and lizards we've been seeing have just as much right to be here as we do."

"I'm still scared of snakes and spiders," Maud insisted.

"Maybe that's because we're just not used to them yet, Maud," Katie said.

"Your mom is right," Gramps added. "I'll bet by this time next Halloween you'll be talking to snakes and spiders like they were your best friends."

"Gramps, you still haven't told us if that was really a ghost," Nora insisted.

"Now that's somethin' I can't answer, partner. But seeing as how there've been folks livin' on this land for hundreds of years,

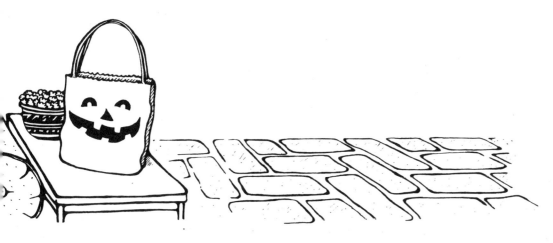

maybe some of 'em decided to stick around awhile to make sure we're taking care of the place."

Later that night, after the rain had stopped, stars shone in a bright, clear sky, and a stillness settled over the desert. Sam and Katie stood on the porch with Gramps. "You know, I never really thought about it, Dad," Sam said, "but maybe there *are* some Anasazi ghosts around here. That's one of the things that makes this place so special, knowing that humans have lived here for so long. We owe it to them to follow the ghost's requests."

Gramps grinned. "Maybe you're goin' to fit in around here after all, Sam."

Before the first light of dawn appeared in the eastern sky, Eya made one last flight over the sleeping people and animals. To complete the Road of Life, she sprinkled a trail of cornmeal around the house and sang: "From the place of the first beginning we have

come. . . . From the Sun Father where our roads come forth."
Pleased with herself, she knew that everyone had found a home in
harmony with each other and the Earth Mother.

"Well, as Gramps would say, it's time to skidaddle!" Eya laughed
a very satisfied laugh and sank back into the earth to join the
ancient ones who would forever live in the spirit of the land.